CURSE of the HAUNTED HOUSE

by Devra Newberger Speregen

illustrated by Anthony Resto

BEARPORT
PUBLISHING

New York, New York

Credits
Cover: © Cary Kalscheuer/Shutterstock and © Sergey Nivens/Shutterstock.

Publisher: Kenn Goin
Editorial Director: Natalie Lunis
Creative Director: Spencer Brinker
Text produced by Scout Books & Media Inc.

Library of Congress Cataloging-in-Publication Data in process at time of publication (2016)
Library of Congress Control Number: 2015020037
ISBN-13: 978-1-62724-806-8

For more information, write to Bearport Publishing Company, Inc., 45 West 21st Street, Suite 3B, New York, New York 10010. Printed in the United States of America.

10 9 8 7 6 5 4 3 2 1

Contents

Good News, Bad News!

CHAPTER 1

On the last day of school, Luke James stepped off the bus and raced through the front door of his house.

"How was your last day, honey?" his mom asked.

"Great," Luke replied. "Fourth grade is over! Hello, summer vacation!"

"Glad to see you're so excited, buddy!" said his dad.

"We're excited, too," said his mom. "While your dad and I love being teachers, we also love getting the whole summer for vacation!"

"So where are we going—to the resort with the giant water slide?" Luke asked hopefully. "I love that place!"

"We're going to Merline, Nebraska," his father replied.

Luke's mouth fell open. "Wait—where?" he asked.

"I know this is a surprise," his father began, "but my grandfather Cornelius died suddenly, and since I'm the oldest

surviving member of the family, I've **inherited** one of his houses in Nebraska. It's been in my family for generations."

"So, we thought it might be a great adventure to spend the summer at the house," said his mother.

"Cool," Luke said with a shrug.

"I've never seen the house," his dad said. "But I've been told it's big, and no one has lived there for years. I've heard strange stories about it all my life, but I've never believed any of them."

Now, thought Luke, *this just might be a very interesting vacation!*

It took two whole days for the family to get to Merline from their home in Boston. When they finally pulled up in front of the three-story house that sat on a **remote** country road, the moon was rising. The house was just as Luke had pictured it: old and creepy. Inside, the furniture was draped  with white cloths to **shield** it from dust. And only some of the lights worked, so the place seemed very dark.

"I'll have to buy light bulbs tomorrow," Luke's father noted, as he turned on his cell phone's flashlight.

"Can I go check out the rooms upstairs?" Luke asked.

"Sure," his father said as he tossed Luke his phone. "You might need this to see."

Luke grabbed his duffle bag and suitcase. As he headed up the creaky staircase, there was suddenly a loud CRRRRAAAACCKKKKKK!

Luke jumped. "What was that?"

"Just the shutters hitting against the side of the house," his father called up the stairs. "Totally normal."

"Yeah, right," Luke muttered. "Totally normal."

Luke put down his suitcase in a large dimly lit bedroom near the top of the stairs. He dumped the contents of his duffle bag onto the bed and grabbed some clothes to put in the closet. By the closet door, he noticed a small framed portrait hanging on the wall. The old man in the picture had a stern, angry expression. *Anderson James* was etched into the metal nameplate on the frame.

"Hmmm . . . Anderson James," Luke mumbled. "Another old relative, I guess."

As he opened the closet door, something leaped out at him. HISS!

Luke gasped and stumbled backward, falling hard against the wall. His heart thumped rapidly as a big, black cat bounced off his chest and ran from the room.

Luke's parents heard the noise and hurried upstairs to see what had happened. They listened as Luke told them about the cat in the closet.

"It's been a long day, honey," his mother said soothingly. "Get ready for bed. You need a good night's sleep."

"We all do," his dad added.

But that night, Luke had a hard time falling asleep. The old house seemed to groan and creak. Tree branches scraped against the windows. The wind whistled through every crack in the building and slammed the shutters against the side of the house.

Luke **burrowed** under his blanket, listening to the unfamiliar sounds. Swish, swish, swish. Just the tree branches blowing in the breeze, Luke told himself as he drifted off to sleep.

Suddenly, Luke found himself running for his life. He was being chased by a huge wolf. Luke ran as fast as he possibly could—through dark hallways, down a steep staircase, and into a damp cellar. He ran faster . . . faster . . . faster . . . until the wolf tackled him. THWUMP!

Luke awoke from the dreadful nightmare, panting, gasping for breath, and drenched in sweat. Then he screamed! The big black cat was sitting on his bed.

In one swift move, Luke grabbed the blanket and pulled it up over his head, pushing the cat off the bed in the process. When he peeked out from under the covers, the cat was nowhere to be found.

CHAPTER 2

Home Alone

Luke opened his eyes as the morning sunlight filled his bedroom. The house was quiet. "Mom? Dad?" Luke called out. No one answered. He looked out the window and saw that the car was gone. Then he noticed a note on his bedside table.

Didn't want to wake you. Went to town to

get groceries. Be back soon. Love, Mom

I hope they remember light bulbs, Luke thought as he **peered** inside the closet. It was empty. No cat. Good.

Relieved, he got dressed. While he waited for his parents to return, he began unpacking his suitcase. Luke scooped up a bunch of clothes and stuffed them onto a shelf in the closet. That's when something fell off the shelf and landed at his feet. It was a large key.

Luke picked up the rusty, old key and turned it over in his hands. "Hmmm . . . I wonder what it's for," he said out loud. "What does it open?"

Luke glanced at the rest of his clothes still in the suitcase, then at the key. His stomach rumbled. He quickly shoved the suitcase under his bed and slipped the key into his pocket.

"I'll finish unpacking later," he said. Then he set off down the stairs to explore—first to find the kitchen for a snack, next to find the keyhole that the mystery key fit into. "I hope this key opens something cool!" he murmured to himself.

At the bottom of the staircase, Luke walked down a long, winding hallway. This wasn't just a house—it was a **mansion**. Soon, he discovered a huge, open kitchen. It was bigger than any kitchen he had ever seen. One wall had several large windows that looked out on a **deserted** country road.

As he gazed out the window, he saw his parents' car approaching—way off in the distance.

"Finally," he exclaimed. "I hope they brought breakfast!"

When he turned to walk out of the kitchen, Luke happened to notice a door with an old keyhole lock. He tried to fit the key in the keyhole. It didn't fit, but Luke discovered the door was already unlocked. Behind it was a huge **pantry**, with shelves from floor to ceiling filled with cans and glass jars and boxes of all kinds of food. The cans were rusty, and the glass jars were filled with dark goo that looked more like a science experiment than food. The boxes were gnawed through and their contents had spilled all over the floor.

Luke stepped inside for a closer look. He pulled a box toward him and opened the top to investigate. A dozen small eyes looked up at him. Then six mice scrambled out, squeaking loudly as they ran across the floor. Luke jumped backwards.

He quickly turned for the door—but it slammed shut, locking him in.

"HEY!" Luke screamed as he flung himself against the door. It wouldn't **budge**. So he banged on it with both fists, hoping his parents had arrived and would come to his rescue. But there was nobody in the house to hear him.

In the dim light of the pantry, he searched the shelves for something that could possibly help him open the door. That's when he saw a pair of scissors on a high shelf. He reached for them just as he felt something else alive in the pantry. It was the big black cat, sitting on the shelf right in front of him.

How did it get in here? It must have slipped in when I did, Luke thought. The cat swiped a paw at Luke.

"Owww!" Luke cried, grabbing his arm. The cat sprang off the shelf and landed on the floor. It glared up at Luke and hissed. Then it disappeared through a small flap at the bottom of the wall next to the pantry door.

Luke followed the cat. He got down on his hands and knees on the dusty floor and squeezed through the flap door into the kitchen.

Luke stood up and started dusting himself off, when he suddenly felt a tap on his shoulder. He let out an ear-shattering shriek.

"What in the world?" exclaimed his startled mom.

"What on earth have you gotten into?" asked his dad, looking at his dust-covered son and shaking his head.

"What took you so long to get back here?" Luke asked, whining a bit. "I saw your car on the road ages ago."

"Well, we were almost home, and then we realized we'd forgotten to get light bulbs," his mom explained.

"So we had to turn around and go back to the store," Dad added. "We thought you'd still be asleep, buddy. But, for goodness sake, what happened?"

CHAPTER 3

Curses and Spells

After Luke told his parents all about the key and the rest of his morning, he went back to exploring the mansion.

"Happy hunting!" said his dad.

Luke was determined to find the keyhole that fit the old rusty key. But by afternoon, he'd had no luck. Frustrated, he took a break from searching and joined his mother, who was sitting on the front porch.

"Don't give up, honey," she said. "You have all summer to solve the mystery of the key."

She poured him a glass of lemonade. "I'll go make us some more," she said, holding up the empty pitcher.

After she left, Luke stook up and stretched as he gazed at the bright blue sky. It was a beautiful day.

"Hey!" a soft voice said.

Startled, Luke spun around to find himself face-to-face with a pale, thin boy standing next to him on the porch steps.

"Wha—? Who are you? Where did you come from? And how come I didn't hear you?" Luke asked, his words tumbling out in a rush.

The boy was thin as a rail, with a head of messy black hair. "My name is Clinton," he replied. "I didn't mean to scare you."

Although Luke was shivering with fear, he said, "You didn't, uh, scare me."

"I came to warn you," Clinton whispered anxiously, leaning in toward Luke so their faces were just inches apart.

Standing this close to the unexpected visitor, Luke suddenly noticed something very strange. Clinton had different colored eyes: one blue and one green.

Luke stuttered. "Um . . . warn me? About what?"

"It may already be too late," Clinton continued. "You and your family should leave right away— before something terrible happens."

"What are you talking about?" Luke asked. "We just got here!"

"There's danger in this house," Clinton whispered. "It started a long time ago, when a farmer named Anderson James lived here."

"Anderson James?" Luke repeated, remembering the portrait in his bedroom. "He must have been a relative of mine. My father said this house has been in the family for generations."

"Anderson James was a horrible man," Clinton went on. "Angry. Miserable. Mean. He ordered everyone around, even his wife and children.

"Then one day, there was a terrible accident. An **electrical storm** caused the house to catch on fire. Everybody made it out except for old Anderson. He didn't die in the fire, but he was badly **disfigured**. After that, he became angrier and meaner than ever. He repaired the damage to the house, but things got so bad, his wife took the kids and left. That's when he discovered magic."

"Magic?" Luke asked, as he noticed the dark clouds that had begun to gather overhead.

Clinton glared at him. "Not magic like card tricks, but evil magic, like witchcraft and **spells**. He locked himself inside

the house and began creating spells and writing them down in a big book. He rarely slept. He didn't eat. He just practiced magic. And then—"

All of a sudden, a powerful flash of lightning lit up the sky overhead. The boy spun around, looking up.

"And then . . . what?" Luke asked Clinton with a shaky voice.

CRACK! A loud clap of thunder shook the porch.

"And then . . . he died," Clinton said, his voice rising. "But not before putting a **curse** on the house."

"A . . . curse?" Luke said with a gulp. "C'mon, that's silly, isn't it?"

Clinton **scowled**. "Everyone in Merline has seen the horrible things that have happened at this house over the years. Everybody believes in the curse."

Luke was shaken. Could there really be things such as curses and spells? "What kind of horrible things?" he finally asked.

"Hauntings!" Clinton shouted over the rumbling thunder and wind rustling all around them. "There are tortured **spirits** trapped in the house. They can **morph** from human into animal form and then back again, and they haunt anyone who enters!"

Luke's eyes widened with fear. Tortured spirits? Morphing animals? What was this strange boy talking about?

Suddenly, a bolt of lightning struck so close to the porch that it knocked both boys over. As they sat up, Clinton whispered close to Luke's ear, "The old man's curse is **activated** by fire or from the energy of big storms—weird storms that come out of nowhere in these parts. Anyone in the house could be in serious danger."

"Anyone?" Luke asked.

"As long as that awful spell book remains hidden somewhere in this house, it isn't safe for any of us!" Clinton said.

Luke's heart was pounding as he struggled to stand. The screen door to the porch squeaked open and Luke turned to see who was there, afraid he'd see a spirit. Phew! It was his mom. "Honey, get inside now before it starts to pour," she said.

When Luke looked back, Clinton was gone.

21

Luke said nothing to his parents about the mysterious appearance of the boy or his strange story. *They'll never believe any of it,* Luke thought.

After lunch, while his parents read quietly on a sofa near a big fireplace in the living room, Luke's curiosity got the better of him. He bravely decided to continue his search for the special keyhole. Maybe he would find the spell book Clinton had mentioned.

So, with the rusty key in one pocket and a cell phone in the other, Luke climbed the rickety steps to the attic. Inside the attic, a dim ray of daylight shone through a small, cracked window. "EEK!" Luke walked into a big cobweb. As he scraped the sticky web off his face, he heard a low, wheezing cough.

"Dad?" Luke said.

"Leave. Get out now!" a raspy, unfamiliar voice commanded. Luke stopped in his tracks.

"Who . . . who's there?" he asked.

Luke peered through the dim light and could see the faint image of an old man. It was more like he could see through the man. But his face . . . his face looked like the old man in the bedroom portrait. Only it was disfigured.

The man scowled. "Leave while you still can!"

"Who . . . who are you?" Luke stammered. "Are you—" Before he could finish, the man disappeared.

Time to get out of the attic! Luke thought as he turned to escape. PLOP! He tripped and fell. He looked up and saw the black cat staring into his face.

Just behind the cat, Luke noticed old yellowed newspaper clippings strewn on the attic floor. He read some of the headlines: "Farmer's Home Believed to Hold Family Curse," "Cursed Farmhouse—Wife Flees with Children . . ."

Luke's mind raced. *Could Clinton's story be true? Is the curse real? Is my family in danger?* he wondered.

CHAPTER 4

Unlocking the Mystery

Luke jumped to his feet and ran down to his bedroom. He slammed the door shut, banging it so hard that the walls shook. CRASH! The portrait of Anderson James fell onto the floor. On the wall where the picture had been was a small square **panel** with a keyhole. *A secret hiding place?* Luke wondered.

When Luke slipped the key into the keyhole, it fit! Then he gave it a turn, and the panel slid open. There was a shelf in the wall that held a large, dusty book. Using both hands, he lifted the heavy book off the shelf. When he brushed the dust off the cover, he read the words *Dark Spells* written in shiny gold letters.

At that moment, a deep rumble of thunder sounded. Luke glanced out the window and saw that the sky was pitch black. CLANG! CLANG! CLANG! Hail began smashing against the metal roof.

Luke's heart began to beat faster. Slowly, he opened the book. There, on the yellowing paper, scrawled in ink, was the name ANDERSON JAMES.

He read out loud what was written just below Anderson's name:

As Luke uttered the last word, he heard a terrifying scream. He could tell the scream came from his father.

Luke dropped the book and raced downstairs, where he found his dad writhing in pain on the living room floor. His head had morphed into that of a wolf!

"What's happening!?" Luke cried out.

His mother, her eyes wide with fright, said, "He started a fire in the fireplace. Then, suddenly, he grabbed his head and screamed!"

From one to another, Luke had read. *From human to animal,* Clinton had warned.

The curse was real!

Luke felt numb. He had read Anderson James's words out loud. Could he have cast a spell on his own father?

"We've got to do something!" his mother pleaded.

Luke looked at the fire in the fireplace. He remembered another part of the curse: "From fire to fire . . ." He had an idea. "I'll be right back."

Luke raced up to his room and grabbed the spell book. By the time he came back to the living room, his father's arms were **sprouting** fur and his fingers were changing into claws!

"From fire to fire!" Luke shouted. Then, with all his strength, he threw the spell book into the flames. The mighty book caught fire, sizzled, and began to burn.

As the book burned, ghostly animal spirits appeared, floating overhead. They transformed into human spirits and then disappeared. Free to rest at last.

"The curse is broken," Luke said breathlessly.

Luke's father looked dazed as he sat up. His head and arms had returned to normal. "What . . . what happened?" he asked.

"Yes—what just happened?" Luke's mother demanded.

"Mom, Dad, it's the house," Luke explained. "It's been cursed for a long, long time!"

Luke told his parents everything—about Clinton, the disfigured man in the attic, finding the keyhole for the mystery key, and discovering Anderson James's terrible book of spells. As he finished his story, Luke felt something brush up against his leg. He glanced down, surprised to see the big black cat snuggling against him.

"Weird," Luke said, puzzled. "Why is the cat being nice all of a sudden?" He carefully picked up the cat and that's when he noticed . . .

The cat had different-colored eyes, one green and one blue. Then he saw the name tag on its collar. It read: CLINTON.

Startled, Luke put the cat down. In a flash, the cat was gone and standing in its place was Clinton.

"W-w-wait . . . ," Luke stammered. "You're the crazy cat?"

"Yes," Clinton confirmed. "Anderson James put a spell on me many years ago. As my page of the book burned, my spirit was set free. Thank you for helping me," he called out as he floated off, like a wisp of air.

Suddenly a gust of wind swept into the fireplace, rustling the ashes of the **smoldering** spell book. The wind blew a few pages from the book—pages that had not burned.

One of the pages floated weightlessly through the air and then landed at Luke's feet.

CRASH! BANG! Jarring sounds **erupted** from the attic above. It sounded like someone throwing things in a rage.

Luke and his parents exchanged terrified glances.

"It's him . . . . It's Anderson James! His evil spirit is still trapped here. Everybody GET OUT of the house!" Luke screamed at the top of his lungs.

The family raced out the door and down the porch steps, just as the sounds in the attic grew louder. Once they were safely inside the car, Luke realized how grateful he was that they had all been able to escape from the cursed mansion with their lives.

Curse of the Haunted House

1. Where do Luke and his family go for their summer vacation, and why do they go there?

2. What is happening in this scene (right) from the story?

3. In the story, Luke meets a boy named Clinton, who tells him the history of the house. Use examples from the story to explain why Clinton tells Luke that his family should leave.

4. Who is Anderson James, and what happened to him?

5. Luke discovers a book in the house. What kind of book is it? Why is it important?

6. Would you like to stay in a haunted house? Explain why you would or would not.

GLOSSARY

activated (AK-tuh-VAY-tuhd) caused by

budge (BUHJ) to move or change position

burrowed (BUHR-ohd) hid beneath

curse (KUHRS) a spell intended to harm

deserted (de-ZUHR-tid) abandoned

disfigured (dys-FIG-yuhrd) to have had one's looks ruined

electrical storm (i-LEK-tri-cul STOHRM) a thunderstorm

erupted (i-RUHPT-id) happened suddenly and violently

inherited (in-HERR-uh-tid) received something, such as money, from someone who has died

mansion (MAN-shuhn) a very large and impressive house

morph (MORF) to gradually change from one thing into something else

panel (PAN-uhl) a thin, flat piece of wood

pantry (PAN-tree) a closet where food is kept

peered (PEERD) looked carefully or curiously

remote (ri-MOHT) far away from other people or things; secluded

scowled (SKOW-uhld) made an angry frown

shield (SHEELD) to protect

smoldering (SMOHL-duhr-ing) burning slowly

spells (SPELZ) words believed to have magical powers

spirits (SPIR-uhts) ghosts

sprouting (SPROWT-ing) growing quickly or suddenly

ABOUT THE AUTHOR

Devra Newberger Speregen is the author of *Tales From The Tomb* and *Scary Stories To Drive You Batty*. She currently writes children's books from her home in Long Beach, New York.

ABOUT THE ILLUSTRATOR

Anthony Resto graduated from the American Academy of Art with a BFA in Watercolor. He has been illustrating children's books, novellas, and comics for six years, and is currently writing his own children's book. His most recent illustrated books include *Happyland: A Tale in Two Parts* and *Oracle of the Flying Badger*. You can find his other illustrated books and fine art works at anthonyresto.com. In his free time, he enjoys restoring his vintage RV and preparing for the zombie apocalypse.